A ghost Story

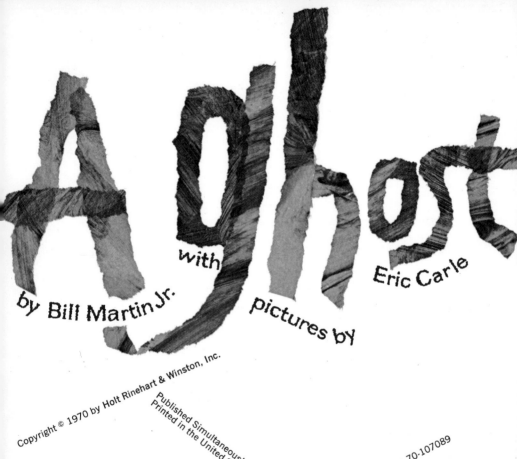

A Ghost

with

by Bill Martin Jr.

pictures by

Eric Carle

Published Simultaneously in Canada
Printed in the United States of America

Library of Congress Catalog No: 70-107089
ISBN: 0-03-084588-2   037   98765432
234567890

Story

and hand lettering by Ray Barber

Holt, Rinehart and Winston, Inc.
New York, Toronto, London, Sydney

In a dark dark woods

there is a dark dark house.

In the dark dark house

there is a dark dark stair.

Down the dark dark stair

there is a dark dark cellar.

In the dark dark cellar

there is a dark dark cupboard.

In the dark dark cupboard

there is a dark dark bottle.

In the dark dark bottle

there is a ghosty ghost.

Slowly slowly the ghosty ghost pushes

out the cork. Now he floats . . . .

.....out of the dark dark bottle

through the dark dark cupboard,

out of the dark dark cupboard

through the dark dark cellar,

out of the dark dark cellar

up the dark dark stair,

out of the dark dark stair

through the dark dark house,

out of the dark dark house

through the dark dark woods,

out of the dark dark woods

into your dark · · · pocket.
dark

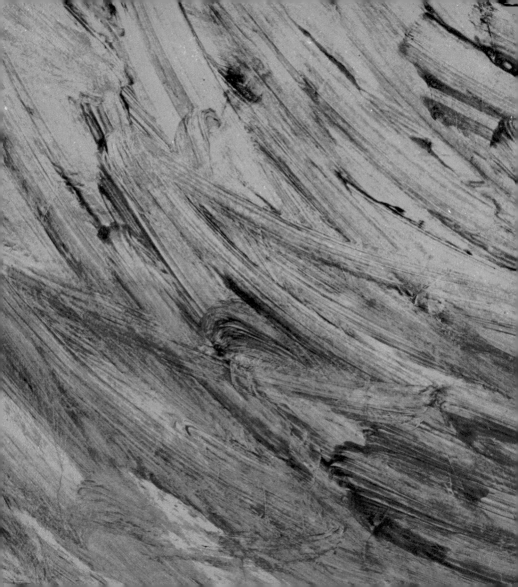